Lucky Socks

For Jack, my inspiration
C.W.

For my parents, my sister, Endaf and Daniel,
for their continuing support and endless patience
C.M.

First published in 2001 in Great Britain by Gullane Children's Books.
This paperback edition published in 2007 by

Gullane Children's Books

an imprint of Alligator Books
Winchester House, 259-269 Old Marylebone Road,
London NW1 5XJ

1 3 5 7 9 10 8 6 4 2

Text © Carrie Weston 2001
Illustrations © Charlotte Middleton 2001

The right of Carrie Weston and Charlotte Middleton to be identified
as the author and illustrator of this work has been asserted by them
in accordance with the Copyright, Designs, and Patents Act, 1988.

A CIP record for this title is available from the British Library.

ISBN-13: 978-1-86233-706-0

Printed and bound in China

Lucky Socks

Carrie Weston

Illustrated by
Charlotte Middleton

GULLANE
CHILDREN'S BOOKS

On Monday morning,
Kevin put on his red socks.

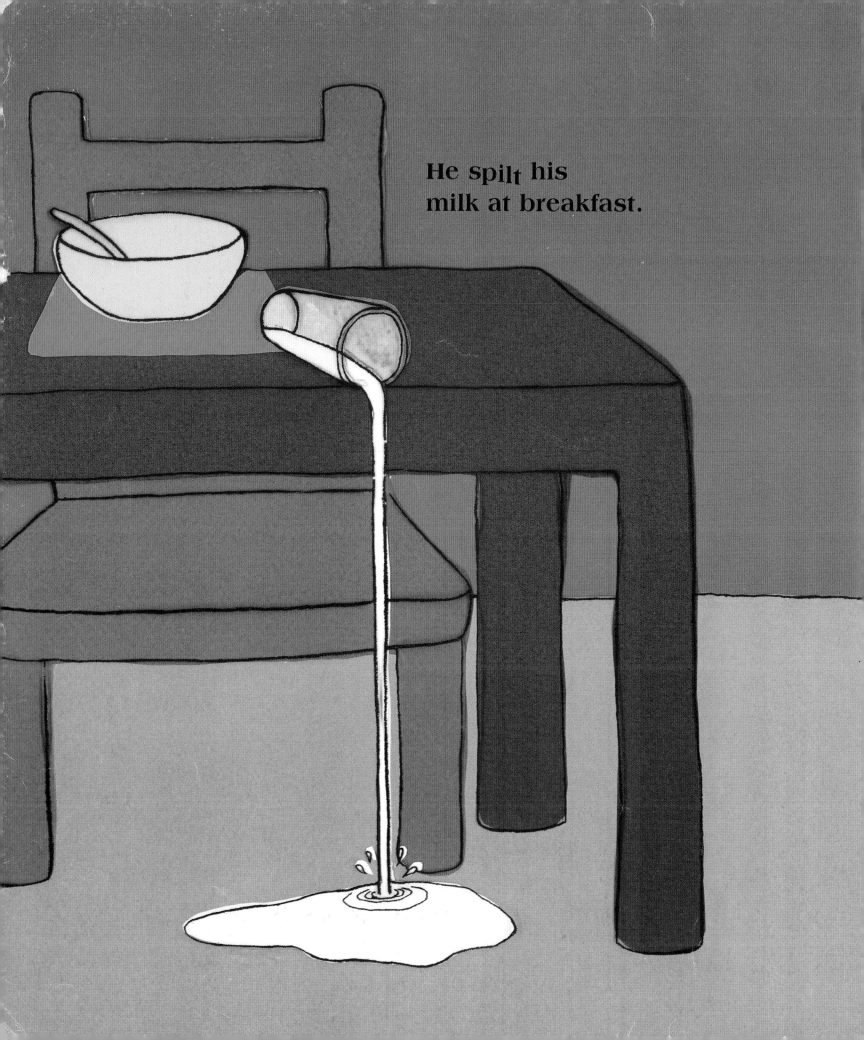

He spilt his
milk at breakfast.

The button
p o p p e d
off his shorts.

And he was late for school.

On Tuesday, Kevin wore his green socks. He got his spelling muddled up at school.

And his bicycle tyre went flat.

On Wednesday,

Kevin wore his blue socks.

It rained all day . . .

. . . and he dropped his sticker collection.

On Thursday,
Kevin wore
his striped
socks . . .

. . . and his beetle escaped
from his bug jar.

There wasn't enough time
for Kevin to have a turn on
the computer . . .

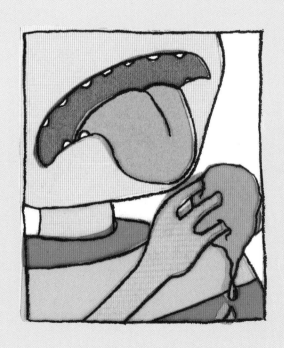

. . . and it was
cabbage and
stew for lunch.

But on Friday,
Kevin wore his
yellow socks.

Mrs Riley chose him
to be the star in the
school play.

The next time Kevin
wore his yellow socks,
Billy Bennet invited him over
to his house to build a tent.
They found ice-cream
in the freezer.

Whenever Kevin had his yellow socks on, his writing always seemed to fit on the page.

Yestarday I went to Billy's howse. We had ize-creem and bilt a tent. Then we looked for bugz in the garden. I fownd tow worms and a sentipeed. Billy fownd a big spider. It waz all hery. We put the bugz in Billys bug jar. Billy sed it wud be a nice surprise for his Mum and Dad. We put the bug jar on the tabel at tee-time. Billy waz rite. His Mum and Dad wer very suprised. <u>By Kevin.</u>

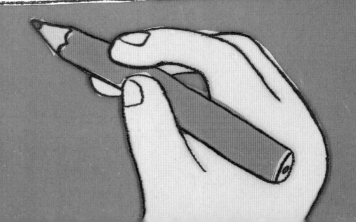

Kevin's ball never went
over the garden fence when he wore
his yellow socks, and he never ever
went home with muddy knees.

But on the morning
of school sports day,
Kevin couldn't find
his yellow socks.

He looked in
the drawer.

He looked in
the cupboard.

He looked
under his bed.

He looked in his bed.

He looked through
the dirty washing.

He even looked
in the fridge.

Kevin's mum helped him to look. She found some red socks, blue socks, some grey socks, spotty socks, tiger-stripe socks, socks with fire engines on, and even Kevin's old baby socks.

"I need my yellow socks!" wailed Kevin.

All Mum could find were some old yellow pants.

Kevin was unhappy
all the way to school.
He was unhappy as he
got changed for sports day.

Kevin fell
flat on his face
in the sack race.

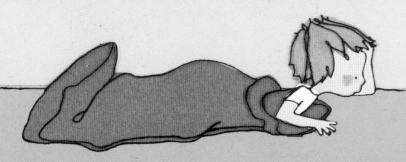

He got all muddled up
in the dressing-up race.

And he just couldn't balance his beanbag

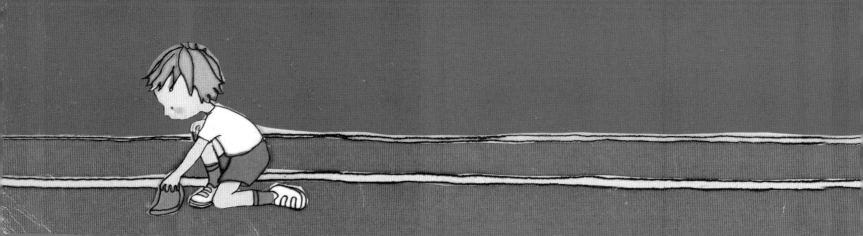

in the balance-the-beanbag-on-your-head race.

Kevin thought about his yellow socks
as the other children went up
to get their medals.

Then Mrs Riley called out Kevin's name . . .

Kevin got a special medal. It was
for trying very hard at everything
– and never giving up! Everyone
cheered and clapped for Kevin.
He felt *really* proud.

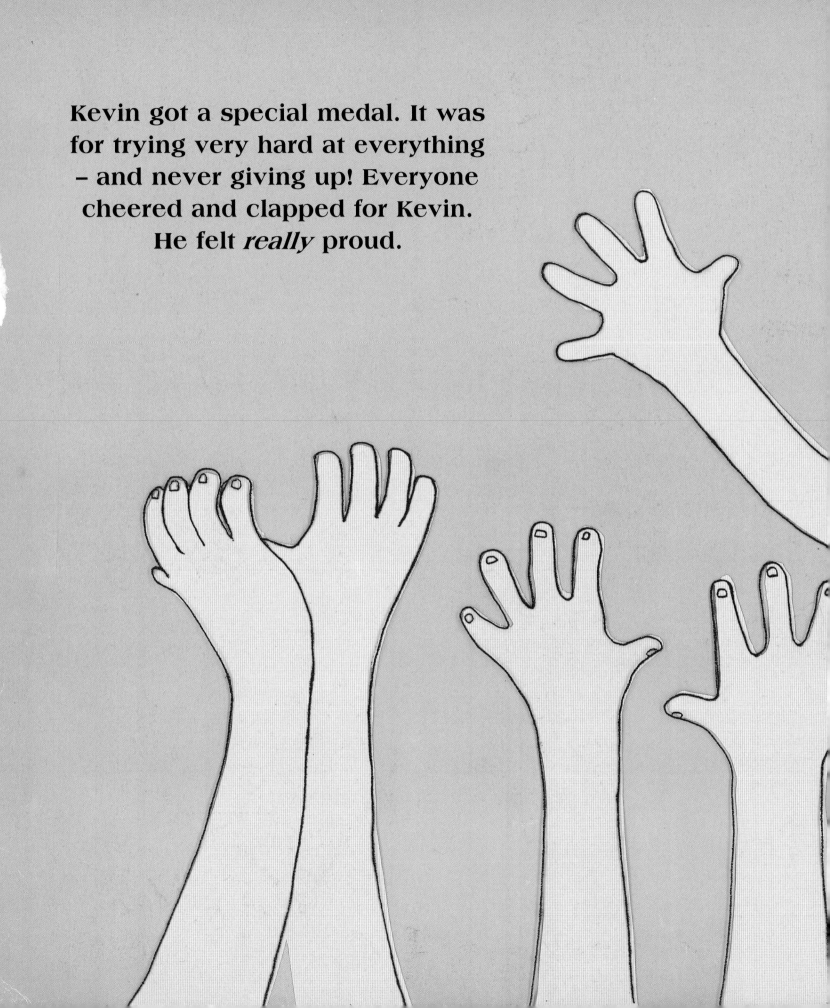

Now Kevin doesn't
mind what colour
socks he wears . . .

But he's very fond of his yellow pants!